D1483169

REX JONES

Alien Attack

by Jonny Zucker

illustrated by Pete Smith

Cover illustration by Marcus Smith

Librarian Reviewer
Marci Peschke
Librarian, Dallas Independent School District
MA Education Reading Specialist, Stephen F. Austin State University
Learning Resources Endorsement, Texas Women's University

Reading Consultant
Mary Evenson
Middle School Teacher, Edina Public Schools, MN
MA in Education, University of Minnesota

STONE ARCH BOOKS
Minneapolis   San Diego

First published in the United States in 2007
by Stone Arch Books,
151 Good Counsel Drive, P.O. Box 669,
Mankato, Minnesota 56002.
www.stonearchbooks.com

Originally published in Great Britain in 2005
by Badger Publishing Ltd.

Original work copyright © 2005 Badger Publishing Ltd
Text copyright © 2005 Jonny Zucker

The right of Jonny Zucker to be identified as the author
of this work has been asserted by him in accordance
with the Copyright, Designs and Patent Act 1988.

Library of Congress Cataloging-in-Publication Data
Zucker, Jonny.
    [Alien Battle]
    Alien Attack / by Jonny Zucker; illustrated by Pete Smith.
    p. cm. — (Keystone Books (Rex Jones))
    Originally published: Great Britain: Badger Publishing Ltd., 2005,
under the title Alien Battle.
    Summary: From a boring science lecture about life on other planets,
fifteen-year-old Rex Jones and his friends, Dave and Carl, are transported
by Rex's mysterious cell phone onto the only space ship that can stop
aliens from destroying planet Earth.
    ISBN-13: 978-1-59889-329-8 (library binding)
    ISBN-10: 1-59889-329-7 (library binding)
    ISBN-13: 978-1-59889-425-7 (paperback)
    ISBN-10: 1-59889-425-0 (paperback)
    [1. Adventure and adventurers—Fiction. 2. Extraterrestrial beings—
Fiction. 3. Space ships—Fiction. 4. Cellular telephones—Fiction.]
I. Smith, Pete, ill. II. Title.
PZ7.Z77925Alc 2007
[Fic]—dc22   2006026731

1 2 3 4 5 6 12 11 10 09 08 07

Printed in the United States of America

Table of Contents

How It All Began

Fifteen-year-old Rex Jones used to have a pretty normal life. He went to school. He hung out with his best friends, Carl and Dave. He played sports. He watched TV. Normal stuff.

Then, a few months ago, Rex bought a new cell phone. It was the last one the store had. Rex had seen the phone in a magazine, but his new phone was different in one way.

It had two extra buttons. One said EXPLORE and one said RETURN. The man in the store said that none of the other phones had those buttons.

The phone worked fine at first. Rex forgot about the extra buttons.

One day the phone started to make a strange buzzing sound. When Rex looked at it, the green EXPLORE button was flashing.

He pressed it, and suddenly found himself in an incredible dream world of adventures. Each adventure could only be ended when Rex's phone buzzed again and the flashing red RETURN button was pressed.

He never knows when an adventure will begin, and he never knows if it will end in time to save him.

< Chapter 1 >

Zapped Into Space

Rex Jones and his two best friends, Carl and Dave, were in Ms. Scott's science class. It was the sleepy part of the afternoon, and everyone was yawning.

Ms. Scott was talking about whether there might be alien life on other planets. Rex felt his phone buzzing. He took it out of his pocket and saw that the green EXPLORE button was flashing.

Carl and Dave saw it too. "Let's get out of here," whispered Rex. He pressed the button.

There was a flash of white light.

The boys found themselves inside the control room of a huge spaceship. There were buttons and levers and lights everywhere. At the front of the control room was a window. The boys could see right into deep, dark space.

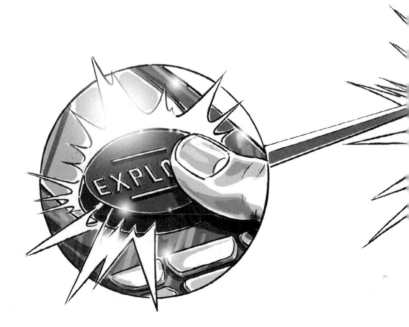

"What are we doing here?" asked Rex, excited.

The screen on the ship's computer flashed a warning.

Planet Earth is at war with several alien armies, it said.

"What's that?" asked Rex. He pointed out the window at a tiny dot that was moving through the stars.

That is a Roltan spaceship, the computer replied.

"The Roltan army is one of the alien armies we're fighting?" Rex asked.

Yes, the screen said.

A printer next to the computer spit out a stack of paper. On the first page was the title: The Roltan Book. Rex flicked through the pages. Inside was a picture of a Roltan fighter with a tiny, gray body and a large, green triangular head.

The Roltans are four inches tall. They are the smallest aliens in the galaxy.

"So that Roltan spaceship is on its way to destroy Earth?" asked Carl. He looked out the window and watched as the dot got bigger and bigger.

The computer blinked. **Yes. They are small, but dangerous. And you three are the only people who can stop them**

< Chapter 2 >

Under Attack

The boys watched as the Roltan
ship came closer and closer. When it
was less than a hundred yards away, it
suddenly fired a red bolt of light at the
ship the boys were in.

The computer flashed.

Laser attack.

Before the boys had time to act, a
laser bolt smashed into the side of the
ship. The whole control room shook.

"Another laser's coming," yelled Dave, looking out of the window.

A second laser bolt crashed into the ship. The boys were thrown across the room. Rex smacked his head against a steel pole.

"Are you okay, Rex?" shouted Carl.

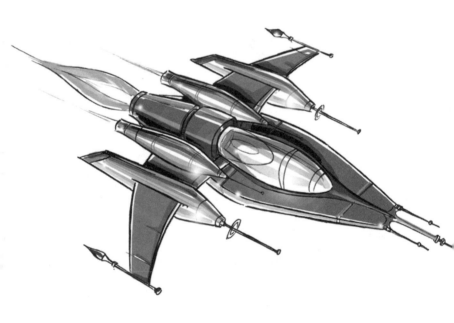

Rex nodded and clenched his fists. "All right," he said. "Let's show them what we can do."

"Yeah!" agreed Carl and Dave.

The three of them ran over to the control panel.

"It's time to fight back!" Rex yelled.

< Chapter 3 >

Roltan Surprise

Each of the three guys pulled a *Fire* lever. Three laser bolts raced toward the Roltan ship.

A ball of fire exploded above the Roltan ship.

"They're in trouble now," said Rex. The Roltan ship moved backward and suddenly vanished.

"I think we scared them off," said Carl.

"But where did they go?" asked Dave.

Carl shrugged his shoulders.

"I don't like it," whispered Rex.

A split second later, they heard a huge thud above them, and their ship was smashed downward.

"What's going on?" yelled Carl.

"They're above us!" screamed Dave.

Somehow the Roltan ship had managed to get on top of the ship that the three were in.

Rex grabbed something on the control panel. It looked like a joystick.

"Do you know what you are doing?" shouted Dave.

"I have no idea," Rex shouted back.

Rex twisted the stick and their ship spun around. Then he powered up the warp drive.

The panel shifted from light speed to warp speed as the ship zoomed forward.

< Chapter 4 >

Space Chase

The ship picked up speed. Soon, the speedometer said it was moving at a thousand miles an hour.

But the Roltan ship was even faster.

Suddenly, it was right in front of them. It sent another laser bolt into the Earth ship. This was the biggest hit.

The boys flew through the air. They crashed against a wall and hit the floor.

The computer flashed.

Engines 1 and 2 have been hit.

"How many engines do we have?" yelled Rex.

Two.

And warp speed has failed.

< Chapter 5 >

Deadlock

"Great!" groaned Rex.

You must attack again, said the computer.

Rex crawled back to the control panel. He pressed *Fire*, but nothing happened.

He pressed it again.

No lasers fired.

"What's happening?" Rex shouted.

Systems are down. No laser power, the ship's computer replied.

"They're going to hit us again," said Dave.

The Roltans have also run out of laser power.

"We're saved!" shouted Dave.

Rex wasn't listening. He was looking out of the window.

The Roltan spaceship was opening up. It looked like the jaws of a crocodile.

The jaws were moving closer and closer to the side of the Earth ship.

"Look!" yelled Rex.

Carl and Dave looked out of the window. "They're going to swallow us up," Dave said. "We're dead!"

Rex looked around, trying to figure out what to do. Suddenly, he noticed a piece of rope on the floor.

"I have an idea," he shouted.

< Chapter 6 >

Space Walk

Rex slid open a small panel in the window. Jets of freezing air blew inside the ship.

"What are you doing?" shouted Carl. He and Dave grabbed a table to stop from flying around.

"Shut the window!" yelled Dave. "You'll be sucked into space!" But Rex didn't listen. Using the rope, he tied his left foot to the ship's control panel.

The Roltan spaceship was right next to the Earth ship.

Rex's body was pulled outside the ship. The rope kept him from flying into deep space.

Rex could see hundreds of Roltan fighter pilots in the cockpit of their ship. They looked exactly like the picture he'd seen in the book.

Rex saw a small blue button on the side of the Roltan ship. He reached out for it, but it was just out of his grasp.

The Roltan fighter pilots stared at him with horror.

Rex pulled himself further forward. His hand reached the blue button.

The Roltan pilots screamed at him.

Rex hit the blue button as hard as he could. Then he dragged himself back inside the Earth ship and slid the window panel shut. Carl and Dave let go of the table.

"What did you just do?" asked Carl.

"I remembered something I saw in that book the computer gave us," Rex explained. "It said there's an emergency *Eject* button on the outside of every Roltan spaceship. Pressing it opens all of their exit panels. It's in case a Roltan is working on the outside of his ship and sees a fire or something else inside."

"But they must have some way of stopping themselves from being ejected," said Dave.

"They know you were the one who pushed it," Carl added.

Rex grinned. "Normally the Roltan on the outside would give a one-minute warning before he pressed the button.

"That warning would give the fighters inside a chance to get their parachutes on, or to bolt themselves down if it's a false alarm and they don't need to leave the ship."

Rex pointed to the window. The three of them watched as red exit panels suddenly opened all over the surface of the Roltan spaceship.

A second later, thousands and thousands of Roltan fighters began flying out of the exit panels. They tried to hold on to their spaceship, but it was no use.

None of them had parachutes on. The sky was filled with desperate Roltan fighters. They screamed in strange, high voices as they floated away into space.

Rex, Carl, and Dave watched as the Roltan fighters became smaller and smaller. After ten minutes they had all vanished.

< Chapter 7 >

More Aliens

Rex opened the ship's food duplicator and found a bottle of water. He poured three glasses, kept one for himself and handed the other two to Carl and Dave. "Here's to winning the alien battle!" he cheered, holding up his glass.

Carl and Dave held up their glasses too. The three of them were about to drink their water when the computer flashed.

More aliens are on their way to attack you.

"Who are they?" shouted Rex.

Timbrans. They know what you did to the Roltans.

Rex laughed. "After the Roltans, the Timbrans should be easy," he said.

The Timbrans are twenty feet tall. Each one of them is as strong as one hundred humans. They are the largest aliens in the galaxy.

The grin left Rex's face.

The three friends looked out of the window as hundreds of Timbran spaceships came into view. They were flying toward the Earth ship at incredible speed.

ALERT

-TIMBRAN_

-
-
-STATUS:-
-CODE RED
-IDENTITY MATCH...

Just then, Rex's phone buzzed. The red RETURN button started flashing.

"Should I?" asked Rex.

"Hurry up!" yelled Dave.

Rex pressed the button.

There was a flash of light and the three boys found themselves back in science class, listening to Ms. Scott.

"If there are aliens, I bet they are friendly, like we are," she said. She looked at Rex, Carl, and Dave. "What do you think, boys?"

"You're probably right, Ms. Scott," said Rex with a laugh, "but I wouldn't count on it!"

About the Author

Even as a child, Jonny Zucker wanted to be a writer. Today, he has written more than 30 books. He has also spent time working as a teacher, song writer, and stand-up comedian. Jonny lives in London with his wife and two children.

About Marcus Smith

Marcus Smith says that he started drawing when his mother put a pen in his hand when he was a baby. Smith grew up in Chicago, where he took classes at the world famous Art Institute. In Chicago he also designed band logos and tattoos! He moved west and studied at the Minneapolis College of Art and Design, majoring in both Illustration and Comic Art. As an artist, Smith was "influenced by the land of superheroes, fantasy, horror, and action," and he continues to work in the world of comics.

Glossary

cockpit (KOK-pit)—the area in the front of a plane or ship where the pilot sits

desperate (DESS-pur-it)—someone who will do anything to change their situation

duplicator (DOO-pluh-kay-tur)—a machine that makes copies of objects

eject (i-JEKT)—to push something or someone out

fate (FAYT)—what will happen to someone

galaxy (GAL-uhk-see)—a group of stars and planets; Earth is in the Milky Way galaxy.

incredible (in-KRED-uh-buhl)—amazing

lever (LEV-ur)—a handle used to control a machine

spaceship (SPAYSS-ship)—a spacecraft designed to fly in space

speedometer (spi-DOM-uh-tur)—an instrument that shows how fast a vehicle is traveling

triangular (trye-ANG-gyoo-luhr)—shaped like a triangle

vanished (VAN-ishd)—disappeared suddenly

Discussion Questions

1. Do you believe in aliens? Why or why not?

2. What are some other stories about aliens that you know? Think about movies you've seen, other books you've read, and things you've heard from friends or family. Talk about these stories. How do they help you understand this book?

3. What are some things you'd like to ask an alien if you met one? What would you like to know about their home planet?

Writing Prompts

1. Create your own alien. What's it called? What does it look like? What does it eat? How does it see, smell, hear, and taste? Don't forget to describe its home planet.

2. If you had a cell phone like Rex's, where would you want it to take you? Write about an adventure you'd go on!

3. Write a story from an alien's point of view. What are some strange things an alien would notice about you? What about your hometown, your school, and your family? How would the alien feel if it came to Earth for the first time?

Internet Sites

Do you want to know more about subjects related to this book? Or are you interested in learning about other topics? Then check out FactHound, a fun, easy way to find Internet sites.

Our investigative staff has already sniffed out great sites for you!

Here's how to use FactHound:

1. Visit *www.facthound.com*

2. Select your grade level.

3. To learn more about subjects related to this book, type in the book's ISBN number: **1598893297**.

4. Click the **Fetch It** button.

FactHound will fetch the best Internet sites for you!